The Dinosaur
Wore Sneakers

by Linda Rapacki

To order additional copies of this book, contact:
Xlibris
844-714-8691
www.Xlibris.com
Orders@Xlibris.com

ISBN: 978-1-6641-9366-6 (sc)
ISBN: 978-1-6641-9365-9 (e)

Print information available on the last page

Rev. date: 11/18/2021

Dedicated to my husband Frank and to my extraordinary family and grandkids, who make life move at the speed of light.

Pop looked down at the garden he just planted.
The ground was dotted with little piles.

There were 12 neat rows of vegetables. He planted cucumbers, tomatoes, string beans, peppers, zucchini and eggplants. He dropped the watering can next to the garden and brushed off his pants. Grandma was watching from the kitchen window.

Grandma reminded Pop to take off his sneakers
and leave them by the back door.

Pop loved to watch his garden grow. Every week the plants grew higher and got stronger. But what Pop loved most was when all the grandkids came over to weed, water and feed the growing garden.

Anthony liked to rake the garden.

Charlee and Ava liked to water the plants.

after Frankie and Marcus filled up the watering cans.

Ryan and Theo liked to count the bees and butterflies
that liked to visit the garden. But each week they all
waited to see how fast the vegetables would grow
they were all very excited to pick the vegetables
and bring them to Grandma. Sunday dinners
always included something from Pops garden.

Weeks were passing and the garden was growing. The grandkids stopped over for a visit with Pop and Grandma, but they also needed to check on the garden. Suddenly there was lots of yelling and calling for Pop to come quickly to the garden. Something was wrong, there were 2 footprints, BIG FOOTPRINTS!

Anthony pointed to the ground and said it looked
like a rabbit came hopping through.

Charlee said "it must be a deer, because deer like to eat vegetables. Marcus said the footprints looked like a bunch of monkeys jumped in the garden. Frankie grabbed Pops pants leg and said he thought it was frogs, frogs like green leaves. Ava was sure it was a unicorn because the garden looked like a rainbow. Ryan laughed and said it was a very big brown moose. And Theo clapped his hands and giggled and said it was an elephant!

Pop listened and laughed out loud. Anthony, Charlee, Marcus, Frankie, Ryan, Ava and Theo begged Pop to tell them what was making those footprints. But first, Pop made them promise not to tell anyone what he saw. They all got very, very quiet and they listened.

Pop told them that it was a dinosaur! A dinosaur wearing sneaker's!!

All of the grandkids fell on the ground and started laughing. They just couldn't believe it. Pop really, really Pop? Are you sure really sure the dinosaur was wearing sneakers? They all looked at each other and then all at once they asked Pop, "do Dinosaur's really wear sneakers? Pop just smiled and looked at towards the back door where he left his dirty sneakers...maybe they do?

The end

Anthony

Frankie

Charlee   Marcus

Ava

Ryan

Theo

Printed in the United States
by Baker & Taylor Publisher Services